# Boys Are Awesome

## A COLLECTION OF SHORT STORIES FOR BOYS

# Hannah Lowe

# TABLE OF CONTENTS

# STORY ONE

# RANDY THOMPSON GAINS HIS CONFIDENCE

Randy Thompson stood in his back yard. Randy was best example of an eight-year-old boy. He was with his father, Tucker Thompson, practicing ball. Backyard baseball practice was much harder than he thought it would be.

Especially with his father pitching the ball. Randy thought that his father was a thousand times better than he was. Randy hoped he would be as good as the other boys. This was his first year playing baseball, but he had wanted to play for a long time.

The only thing that stopped him was his own self-doubt. He would watch YouTube

videos of Babe Ruth playing ball and knew inside of his heart that he could never measure up to The Great Bambino, and he was right. Randy had flopped his first game.

The coach said he had skills, but he didn't have the confidence to get the job done.

His father threw him another ball. This time he hit the ball of the tip of his bat, fouling it. Perhaps he could do this after all. Only time would really tell.

Randy and his father walked back to the shed to put away his baseball gear. He knew his parents had paid a small fortune to allow him to play. They had bought him the best gear, the best shoes, but that wasn't what mattered. His parents had told him that it was the heart and soul that mattered.

And the fun. His father had told him to make sure he had lots of fun.

"Good practice, son. You will do great in the next game, I know it. Just don't let yourself fear failure, have fun, and make friends. That's all any of the boys on your team could hope for," Tucker smiled down at his son. "After all, it's only your first year. I have seen you hit a whopper during backyard ball, I know you can do it."

"But people aren't watching me in the backyard," Randy said.

"Just imagine it's just you out there, and do the best you can," his father added.

"And if we win?" Randy asked with a sly smile.

"Then all the better," Randy's father

patted him on the back as he smiled back.

They made their way into the house and could smell Randy's mother Caroline's cooking coming from the kitchen.

"Just remember son," his father said, as he closed the door, and they took off their muddy cleats together. "Never let the fear of striking out keep you from playing the game. Do you know who said that?"

"Babe Ruth, duh, dad," Randy nudged his father.

"Supper's ready," Caroline called from the kitchen.

They both came running to the dinner table, half starved, and exhausted.

Next Saturday, the game had started and was nearly over. It was hot and a cool summer rain shower had come rained down on the field but there was no lighting. It was the perfect playing weather.

Randy stepped up to bat and took a deep breath. His father had worked with him ten times since the last game. Randy's father knew what he was talking about, he was his assistant coach after all. But Randy didn't know if he could do what it took to help win the game.

They were tied and at the bottom of the ninth inning, two outs for Randy's team, and Billy Blackwood was pitching. He was the best pitcher in town. Randy was sitting at a strike and two balls. The basses were loaded.

He just knew he was going to disappoint his team.

Billy took a breath, and Randy kept his eyes on the ball, but then the crowd was there too. Before he knew it, the Ump called another strike. Randy had two strikes, two balls, and not a hope or prayer to win this game.

Then, Randy remembered what his father had told him, what his mother had said, and how his head coach had encouraged him. He needed confidence.

Randy took a breath and made the crowd go away in his mind. Now, it was just him and Billy. He saw Billy take a breath, pitch, and release. The ball was just outside.

Randy stood still as the Ump called ball

three.

Randy took a breath, he had to do this for him and his team. He stood tall and smiled as he felt confidence well up in him. Randy lifted his bat like The Babe had and pointed to the outfield with it.

He got in place, pushed the crowd away in his mind once more, and smiled as Billy released the ball again. Randy swung the bat as he heard the crack of it vibrate in his ear. He dropped the bat and ran, not caring if the ball was foul or not.

Randy ran to first as Jason Lane ran home. He made it to second as Ryder Smith reached home plate. Then his foot hit third, as Cole Carmicle scored a point.

Out of the corner of his eye, he saw the ball flying back in field as he ran home. Three quarters of the way, Randy slid until his foot hit home plate, just seconds before the catcher caught the ball.

He had found confidence and his team had won.

If Randy had learned anything else that day, it was that by having heroes like The Great Bambino, he could make it in the world of baseball. If he was only a fraction as good as The Great Bambino was, then everything would be just fine.

# STORY TWO

# BARRY THE DINOSAUR LEARNS TO BE BRAVE

Barry was on a scenic walk with his other dinosaur friends. He was a little anxious as he didn't go out often. Barry had found himself in a unending anxious loop. Every time he left the house, he was scared something bad would happen. He was scared something bad would happen because he didn't leave the house often. Barry didn't leave the house due to this fear. He slowed down a little. He was becoming spooked by a strange-looking tree in the distance.

" Barry?" One of his friends turned around to look at him, "what are you afraid of this time?"

" Barry is afraid of everything," another one of his friends added.

"Don't be mean."

"There's a figure, that way..." Barry pointed his hand towards the weird tree.
One of the dinosaurs sniggered, "That's a tree, look!" They kicked the tree, it didn't even budge, "see, it's not going to hurt you."

Barry gulped and took a step forward.
"Kick it too! Be brave, Barry. You'll never get anywhere if you don't face your fears."
Barry nervously continued to take steps towards the tree until it was right in front of him. Now that he was close to it, it wasn't so scary.

He could clearly tell that it was just a lame tree. He used his leg to kick the tree as hard as she could.

"See!"

"You're right, it's just a tree."

"You have nothing to be scared of when you're with us," another dinosaur said proudly.

Barry nodded, "you're right."

They all continued walking through the forest when a strange-looking fruit fell in front of them.

"Monster!" Barry cried out and rushed to hide behind one of his friends.

"Are you kidding me? It's just a weird looking apple. Barry, you're so silly," she kicked the apple over to him, "taste it."

Barry stared at the thing in front of him. An apple, he had never tasted an apple before.

The thought of trying something new scared him. What if he hated it?

"You'll like it, just give it a try. You don't have to have it again if you hate it."

"I supposed you're right," Barry lowered his head down and took a bite out of the apple. He felt the strange texture in his mouth and immediately stopped chewing. He looked nervously at his friends.

"Chew it..."

Barry began to chew the apple, feeling the juices flow all around his mouth. He finished chewing.

"Did you enjoy it?"

"I loved it!" Barry eagerly took another bite, and another, until the apple was gone.

"See! Sometimes trying new things and being courageous is good!"

Barry agreed with her. By being brave, he had tried out a new flavor, which he loved. He had even overcome his fear of strange looking trees in the woods.

"I'm going to try and be more courageous," Barry said confidently as he headed to front of the pack.

"That's great!"

Barry led his friends, kicking any weird trees and trying out all sorts of new fruits and vegetables. He especially liked raspberries now, which was fun because they matched his name almost perfectly.

Barry felt successful, he had overcome his fear of going outside just by being courageous and having some help from his friends. Of course, there were some things he didn't like, but those discoveries were all part of the fun, too.

" Barry! Come and try these berries!" One of his friends called him over to a berry bush. It had a bunch of blackberries all over it.

Barry leaned into the bush and bit a few off, chewing them in his mouth, not hesitating for a single second.

"Did you like them?"
His friend said excitedly, "they're my favorite!"
"I love them!" Barry pulled off more berries to eat.

Barry you're so much more fun now! We should go out all the time," another unicorn said to him.

"How about tomorrow?"

Barry found himself arranging plans for once, he was having was more fun than usual and even getting a little ahead of himself.

"Tomorrow it is!"

# STORY THREE

# JOSEPH'S SECRET

Joseph Loudermilk was a good boy. He was only eight but he had done everything he could to stay a good boy. He did his chores, listened to his parents, and even made good grades as a third grader. But he didn't like to do much away from his parents for a good reason. It was hard for him to feel comfortable about leaving them, overnight especially.

On Monday, his friend Liam had invited him over for a birthday sleepover the next Friday night after school. There was promised to be some fun things at the party, and Joseph could even stay and play games and swim on Saturday until late.

But Joseph didn't know if he could make it through the night, let alone all day the next day.

After receiving the invitation that day at school, Joseph went home to his parents.

"How was your day today?"
His mother asked him as she sat at her desk in the living room going over budgets for her restaurant.

"Fine," was all Joseph said, he had no plans to tell his parents about the invitation. With any luck, the weekend would come and go, and he could make up some fib to tell Liam on Monday morning as to why he couldn't make it to his sleepover. But then he felt bad, he just knew that he couldn't do it, but he wasn't a liar either.

That next Thursday night, Joseph was sitting on the floor putting a Lego castle together when his father walked into his room. Joseph had done a good job keeping the sleepover a secret and was only a day away from missing it, but all the while he had tried to figure out how he was going to get out of it without telling a lie.

"Can we have a talk, Joseph?"
His father asked him, as he sat on the floor in front of him.

"Okay, dad, what's up?"
Joseph asked him. But then he saw the invitation in his father's hand.

"Your mother found this in your backpack when she was going through your leave at home papers. Why haven't you said anything about this? Liam is your best friend," He asked his son.

"Because I'm not sure that I want to go," Joseph said with a frown on his face as he took the invitation from his father.

"Why not? This is the first big boy party you have been invited to."

"You know why not. I have never even stayed at Aunt Jill's house before because of my secret. I don't want Liam and half the boys in my class to know my secret," Joseph said with an even bigger frown. "I want to go, but I'm scared."

"All you need is some courage," his father said to him. "If you have courage, you can go, and nobody will know about the fact that you still wet the bed sometimes at night.

It's not uncommon for little boys and girls to have issues as they get older. It will get better, but you still can go and have fun."

"But how?" Joseph asked.

"Just make sure that you don't talk about it if you don't want to. Go into the bathroom when you get ready for bed, and nobody will know that you have to put on night time underpants to go to sleep. Then you can take a bag with you and put the underpants into in the morning. Then you can put the bag in your suitcase to throw away at home. See, easy peasy!"

"I guess," Joseph said, but this time he had a smile on his face. "I think I'm going to go! And maybe, if I have enough courage, I will tell Liam about my secret."

Friday, at the end of the school day, Joseph was supposed to go home with Liam to start the sleepover. The fact that he was keeping a secret from his best friend was bothering him. But Joseph didn't know if this was a secret that he wanted to keep to himself or share with his friend.

As the bell rang to end the day, he pulled Liam aside before walking to the vehicle.

"I need to tell you something," Joseph said as he looked his best friend in the eyes.

"What?" Liam said.

"I almost didn't want to come to your sleepover tonight," Joseph admitted sadly.

"Why not?" Liam asked as though he had done something wrong.

27

Joseph took a breath to try to find the courage to tell his friend what he wanted to tell him. He knew his father said he didn't have to, his father had even given him advice how to keep it a secret. But he felt like his friend Liam, if he was a good friend, would be on his side no matter what.

"I have accidents sometimes in the night, and I have to wear night time underpants too," Joseph said as he looked down and then back up to his friend.

"Really?" Liam squealed a little, which made Joseph nervous. "So do I! And my mother told me how to take care of things without the other boys knowing, but if they say anything to you or to me about it, I will always be your friend! Now let's go have fun!"

Joseph was in shock. He had no idea his best friend had the same problem he did. Finding the courage to tell the truth took a lot, but now that he had been honest, Joseph felt that much better. As he made his way to the car with Liam to have the best sleepover ever, he felt the courage within him. If any of the other boys asked him about his problem, he knew he could be honest and defend himself and Liam if need be.

His father had been right, and Joseph knew that he could be courageous always, now that he had told the truth about the hardest thing he had to face, yet.

# STORY
# FOUR

# PEGGY THE PEGASUS

Peggy the Pegasus sighed. She had been trying to perfect her flying all day but had failed to do so every time. It was beginning to make her sad. All of her friends could fly by now, except for her.

"Peggy, did you learn to fly yet?" One of her friends asked as she landed beside her. She had been flying around all day.

Peggy shook her head, "It's so difficult how do you do it?"

"Like this!" She flapped her wings and lifted off the ground, "just think about what you want your wings to do and they'll do it just like moving a body part."

Peggy tried it out, but her wings just refused to move, "I can't do it."

"Don't be so negative! I have to join the others but I'm sure you'll get it eventually. Good luck!" She flew off into the sky, reuniting with her friends.

Peggy went to go and see her grandfather, maybe he would be able to help her with her problem. After all, he was a great flyer.

"Peggy, I'm glad to see you," he noticed Peggy's presence before he had even seen her "what brings you here today?"

Peggy was nervous, she was embarrassed about her problem.
"Grandfather, I can't fly. It's so embarrassing all of my friends can and I just... Can't."

"I see," he chuckled a little, "you need to stop thinking that you can't and believe that you can. Trust me."

"That doesn't make any sense, this is impossible..."

"It's not impossible, every other pegasus has to go through it too."

"Then how come it's so much easier for them!"

"It's easier for some than others, just believe in yourself. You'll get there eventually."

Peggy shook her head, "Do you really think I'll be able to fly?"

"I know you can do it, now go and practice!" Her grandfather ushered her out of the room.

Peggy stood outside again, repeating to himself, "I can do this... I can do this..." She pushed any negative thoughts out of her mind and began believing that she could fly, just like every other pegasus out there. She flapped her wings, gently at first then speeding up the pace, still repeating the words as she concentrated on moving her wings.

"I can do this."

She slowly felt herself lift off the ground. She kept thinking about it, believing in herself that she could go higher. And that's exactly what happened, she flew higher and higher and higher.

"I did it!" She let out an excited cry and happily flew over to her friends, excited to show them that she had finally mastered flying.

"You're flying Peggy!" They shouted, "you can finally play with us!"

"I can! What game are you playing?"

"Tag!" Her friend gently patted her with her foot, "and you're it!"

Peggy chased her friends around the skies. Her grandfather came out to check on her and saw her happily soaring through the skies. He had a huge smile on his face.

# STORY FIVE

# KINDNESS IS CONTAGIOUS

Tommy was only seven when he had to go into the foster care system. He had never heard of what foster care was or what adoption was, but when his parents could no longer take care of him, he was sent to a foster family. It wasn't that his parents had done anything bad, they simply went to a better place.

Tommy didn't have any other family, so he got to meet Mama K and Papa C.
Mama K and Papa C where the sweetest people. They made him feel welcome right away, but he missed his mother and father dearly. Mama K and Papa C knew that Tommy

would miss his parents and made sure to allow him to talk about them as often as he could.

On his first night there, Mama K read him a bedtime story and talked to him about all the kinds of love. She said that it was something that she often read to the kiddos that came through their house. It helped to make them understand what was going on.

"Sometimes kids have one parent sometimes they have two. Sometimes their parents have different skin colors than they do, sometimes they have the same. Sometime children look exactly like their parents sometimes they look different. There is foster care, adoption, and more to help take care of kiddos that can no longer stay at home, like you," she smiled at him. "Sometimes it's hard to understand just exactly why this has happened, but you should know that Papa C and I are always going to be here for you."

Tommy didn't know what to say to her. He rolled over and went to sleep as tears rolled down his cheeks.

*Eventually*

A little over a year later, Tommy, Mama K, and Papa C we're standing in a courtroom. This was a room where a judge talked to people about important things.

At the end of the appointment, Mama K and Papa C adopted Tommy. All their friends and family cheered as the judge called him theirs. Tommy was happy, he didn't forget his mother and father. Tommy had not moved past their love, he only added love on top of it. Mama K and Papa C had so much kindness in their hearts that they took him in and made him their own.

Eventually, the couple took in another child, another little boy just two years younger than Tommy. His name was Garrett and he and Tommy became the best of friends.

*Kindness is Contagious.*

Tommy and Garrett became close. They were like brothers almost instantly. Mama K and Papa C we're both pleased with the kindness that he had shown the younger boy. It was the same kind of kindness that they had shown Tommy when he first arrived.

Tommy played a big part in reading the story to Garrett that had been read to him on his first night in the home of Mama K and Papa C. He just added some words! Mostly words about his experience and how kindness was the most important thing to him.

The kindness that two strangers had bestowed upon a little boy was contagious and spread to another. A little under a year later, Garret became Tommy's for real brother. They were a happy and healthy family, but none of it could have been possible without kindness at the heart of it all.

# STORY SIX

# THE UNGRATEFUL FAIRY

"Urgh! This sucks!" Angela the fairy threw away yet another gift from one of her fans. It was so difficult being a popular singer like her, everyone would always send you bad gifts that were nothing but a waste of space.

"You should appreciate your gifts more, you know. One day you may regret it," her mother pulled the gift out of the bin and looked at it. The gift was a candle set. It looked pretty expensive too.

"This is nice, why don't you like it?"

"I hate the color orange," she frowned. Her mother put her nose up to the packaging and breathed in the candle, "but it smells very

nice. They'll make your room smell good."

"I guess you're right... But still!" Angela took the candles from her mother, giving them a sniff, "they do smell good."

"You need to be more grateful, Angela," her mother fluttered her wings and sighed sadly. "You're so lucky compared to other fairies."

Angela gulped as she opened another gift, it was a purple blanket. The color matched her hair and it was very fluffy. She loved it.

"This is great, people like this are the reason I love getting gifts," Angela hugged the blanket to her chest and buried her head in it, "smells brand new."

Her mother shook her head and left the room, leaving Angela to do whatever she wanted.

A couple of days passed and Angela continued to receive more and more gifts. Until one day, people stopped sending them altogether. This was confusing, she usually received tons.

"Mother, have we had any post recently?" Angela asked, she thought maybe her mother was keeping it from her to make her appreciate the gifts more.

Her mother shook her head, "none, did you tell people to stop sending them?"

"No..." Angela gulped, maybe she had messed this up for herself.

"Strange."
Angela nodded and headed outside, deciding to go on a short walk. Maybe her fans would

notice her and give her some attention.

She wandered the streets and people gave her attention, but it wasn't good attention. People frowned at her, others tutted and whispered to their friends. Angela was utterly confused.

Angela and had enough of the stares and whispers about her and started to head home, prepared to just sleep it off and pray this was all a bad dream until she heard someone say.

"That's Angela, the singer who throws all of her fan's gifts away."

Angela froze, so this is why everyone here seemed to dislike her, they knew about everything she did at home. She immediately regretted it, she should have appreciated the gifts more, now everyone hated her!

"How do you know that?" Angela called after the girl who said it.

The girl scoffed, "There's a video of you throwing some candles away, I'm surprised you haven't seen it already," she walked away, leaving Angela alone in the street.

She gulped and began to fly home, who could have taken that video? Her mother was waiting for it at home.

"I'm guessing you heard about the video?"

Angela nodded sadly, "I'm so sorry."

"It's not me you should be saying sorry to right now," her mother sighed.

"You're right, I'm going to go and fix this. Angela rushed outside yet again, picking u speed and lifting off the ground using he wings. She headed to a busy shopping center and called for everyone's attention.

"Guys!"

Everyone turned to look at her. They looked pretty angry, to say the least.

"I want to say something. I'm sorry for everything. This whole thing has taught me that I really need to learn to appreciate things more. I've done some really bad things and I'd just like to say sorry to all of you, I'll understand if you don't want to support me anymore. Just know that I'm sorry. And I promise I'll appreciate you all from now on."

Angela headed home, and the next day she was awoken with the familiar call: "Angela! You have post!"

# STORY SEVEN

# JERRY THE RABBIT LEARNS TO LOVE HIMSELF

Jerry the rabbit sat hidden behind his hutch, watching as all of his brothers and sisters got attention from a bunch of different people. Jerry took a look at himself. His fur wasn't one solid color like everyone else's fur. He had lots of different colored spots all over him. The way his fur looked made him very insecure. He was so insecure that he even felt nervous around his friends. Why couldn't he be like his brothers and sisters? Brown, white or black? He wondered to himself. Why did he have to be all three? The colors all mixed together in a way that looked strange to him. Black dots, brown dots, white dots. These

colors didn't even go together! Every time new people would visit, he would always hide, making sure they wouldn't see what he looked like. He had made up countless excuses by now. He was always 'too tired', 'eating', or

something along the lines of that.

He was way too different from everyone else. Why would they want to see him over his amazing brothers and sisters? Not receiving any attention in a crowd that size would just be embarrassing and he knew that's exactly how the event would play out. That would for sure make him feel worse, so he just never joined in on the action.

One of his sisters noticed him sitting out and approached him. She was a pure white, beautiful rabbit and usually ended up being the favorite since she was so friendly.

"Jerry, what are you doing behind here?" she asked him, looking around to see if there was anyone else around.

"I'm just... napping," Jerry lied, not wanting to tell her the truth behind why he was here.

"Then why are you awake? Come and get attention from the strangers! It's fun, you'l enjoy it."

"I'm alright here, attention is tiring, Jerry gave her a small, weak smile.

"It's not tiring at all, what's the matter? She looked sad, "I'll stay with you if you like.

"You can keep the attention to yoursel: Those people will all love you way more tha. me."

"Why will they prefer us?" She shook her head, "I don't think that's true at all, everyone is all fairly similar. We are all related after all."

"All of you are similar, yes. But look at my fur compared to yours... It's so gross," Jerry huffed and turned his head away from her, not wanting her to see his sad face.

"You don't like your own fur?" She tilted her head to the side and furrowed her brow, "that's strange."

"I hate it. I wish I looked like everyone else," Jerry took another look at his family. They all looked wonderful. One of his brothers was black, one of them brown. Their fur looked so soft and shiny when it was out in the sun.

"You're different, and that's a good thing,"

she took a good look at him, "your fur is so pretty. I'd love to have fur like that."

Jerry was confused. Why would someone who was as perfect as her want to look like him?

"Why would you want this? Your fur is amazing?"

"It's pretty, but it's also basic. Almost every bunny in the world has fur like me. You're part of a small amount that looks different, so you should embrace it with open paws!"

"They won't like me, please just let me be alone for a while. Maybe I'll join you next time."

"They will like you! Look, I'll prove it to you, come with me and you'll see how much these people will like you. Just for being a little different."

"Why would they like me over you guys?"

"You're unique, people love that."

Jerry gulped.

"Fine then."

His sister led him out from behind the hutch. Everyone turned to stare at him. He knew this would happen, they were definitely judging him for having weird fur.

"Look at this bunny!" A child yelled and rushed over to him, followed by another child.

"His fur is so pretty!" They shouted and squatted down to pet him.

Jerry looked around at all the attention he was receiving. Maybe his sister was right, being unique was good. He chomped his jaws round a carrot he had been given, and right now, his unique fur was definitely working in his favor.

Printed in Great Britain
by Amazon